I'M GLAD I'M NOT AN ALLIGATOR

written by Rita Kayser
illustrated by Lorraine Arthur

© 1983. The STANDARD PUBLISHING Company, Cincinnati, Ohio
Division of STANDEX INTERNATIONAL Corporation. Printed in U.S.A.

The distinctive trade dress of this book is proprietary to Western Publishing Company, Inc., used with permission.

Y0-BUW-898

I'm glad I'm not a spider
Hanging in a web all day.

By the time I got my shoestrings tied
I'd have no time to play!

I'm glad I'm not a rooster
Crowing early every morn.

I'd rather stay all snuggled
In my bed so soft and warm!

I'm glad I'm not an alligator
With so many teeth to brush.

I'd never have time for a bedtime story
Even if I'd rush!

I'm glad I'm not a fish
Swimming day and night.

I wouldn't mind if the food was good,
But worms give me a fright.

I'm glad I'm not a little gray mouse
Hiding here and there.

I couldn't play ball, or roller-skate,
Or wear pretty ribbons in my hair!

I'm glad I'm not a wise, old owl
Sitting in a tree.

I couldn't giggle and tell silly jokes
Or snuggle on Daddy's knee!

I'm glad I'm not an elephant!
Who'd want to be one of those?

I'd carry a trunk wherever I went
And still have no place for my clothes!

There's nothing wrong with any of
 these.
God made them, every one.

But He made me in a special way
In the image of His Son!

I'm just a little person now,
Not famous, rich, or strong.

Sometimes I do a few things
That Mother says are wrong.

But Mother still loves me, and so does
  Dad,
And Granny, and my friends.

They tell me that Jesus loves me, too,
For He died for all our sins.

It's good to know that Jesus loves us,
And that He's always there.

And we can talk to Him anytime
Just by saying a prayer.

God loves me now, and always will.
He made me special, you see!
And I will live in Heaven with Him
For all eternity!